Dani Marie always had a dream to publish a book at age seven and has had her family supporting her all her life. Dani Marie always enjoyed a good scary story or movie. But what inspires her to write is the thrill of the kill. It's exciting, thrilling and intense. But most of all, she enjoys it when the main characters overcome impossible odds.

Robert Quinto grew up watching horror movies such as horror slashers…but he also watched other types of scary movies while he grew up, each one intriguing him more than the last…until he really knew how to get under people's skin when it came to saying the right words to give people chills. Now he wants to give terror a name, a name that movie monsters will fear when they hear his name and a horror like no other. This is only the beginning…

Dedicating this book to my mom and fiancé who always supported me.

I am dedicating this book mostly to my fiancé whom I support a lot and I will continue to do so for the rest of my life. Also my mom and my stepdad who have supported me as well as my dad, my stepmom and my brothers, thank you for everything.

**Dani Marie and
Robert Quinto**

# DARK INTENTIONS

AUSTIN MACAULEY PUBLISHERS™
LONDON • CAMBRIDGE • NEW YORK • SHARJAH

**Ordering Information:**
Quantity sales: special discounts are available on quantity purchases by corporations, associations, and others. For details, contact the publisher at the address below.

**Publisher's Cataloging-in-Publication data**
Marie, Dani and Quinto, Robert
Dark Intentions

ISBN 9781647502096 (Paperback)
ISBN 9781647502089 (Hardback)
ISBN 9781647502102 (ePub e-book)

Library of Congress Control Number: 2020914249

www.austinmacauley.com/us

First Published (2020)
Austin Macauley Publishers LLC
40 Wall Street, 28th Floor
New York, NY 10005
USA

mail-usa@austinmacauley.com
+1 (646) 5125767

We thank Austin Macauley Publishers for the opportunity
to get our work published.

# The Intro

The stories people tell one another are supposed to scare you and frighten you about the littlest things; but maybe, that is because no one believed that they were true. But what if some stories were true? What if I told *you* a story about a man named Marcus Slayer, who would bring absolute fear into your life? But instead of saying all of these words to you, allow me to tell you a story about Marcus Slayer and the horror he brought to people everywhere. No one was safe from his wrath as long as Marcus ran free throughout the streets of Clouds-dale. But this recent tale I will tell you as to how Marcus was disarmed and weakened and how he regained the book of spells known as *Dark Power*, and how he had his weapons of mass murder returned to him. Leading to a tale of horrific events, and if he should find you…pray to the God you wish; and he will send thee to whom you chose.

Now let us begin this tale of *Dark Intentions*.

# Chapter 1

## Beginning Intentions

The story starts on June 10, 1988, with a town called Clouds-dale as it has always been a nice town that has some of the best education you could ask for; from Clouds-dale university.

Where a class is taking place at this moment. Professor Hank was the teacher of this class, as he was telling the students that he had a special assignment for them, as it would require eight students for this task. The students were very curious about this task, as one student named Jack asked what it was. Professor Hank said it is a task to find hidden secrets about the town of Clouds-dale, to see what mysteries lie deep beneath the town, and what it is hiding from the rest of the world. Professor Hank picked ten students, starting with Jack, who was the boy who asked the question before. Jack came down to the front of the class as did Jennifer, Bobby, Calvin, Selena, Frank, Judy, Kelly, Roland, and Sandy, as they all were chosen for this project. Class was over as the professor took the kids in the back and told them their assignment and to see what interesting things, they could find hidden in the town. The professor gave them two weeks for the project, so they started right away as they went on their computers and started looking up anything they could get on the town that may have a secret or two. Jack managed to find something on a man named Marcus Slayer, who apparently murdered a lot of people back in the day, using powerful magical spells to kill his victims. Jack told the other guys and girls about this and right away, they seemed interested about this information. To know that no one talks about Marcus Slayer anymore because no one has ever heard of him; plus, it was the only thing they could find that was even remotely exciting. Jack took his car, as well as Selena and Roland took their car, and car pooled with the rest of the students, as they were headed for a place called Shadow Lake; to a building with old records on Marcus Slayer. Jack and the others had arrived as the sky was getting pretty dark. Jack and the others headed towards the building—they were starting to get a little scared—and as they went in the old building, they saw all the filing cabinets that were there around the office. The crew started to look through the filing cabinets to see where the files on Marcus Slayer were, so they get a good grade on the project, and what they found was not only interesting, but terrifying. Bobby found a file stating that Marcus Slayer is not only secret to the town of Clouds-dale, but he is still alive and lives not far from where the kids were. Bobby found out that Marcus also had a sister that was still alive, and with someone named Thomas Mayfield. So, they found the sisters address to see what information they could gather on.

Marcus Slayer. Katherine has not heard the name *Marcus* in a long time and wanted to keep it that way; but all that was about to change, when she heard her doorbell ring. The kids were at the door with Jack up front as he saw Katherine open the door. "Hello, can I help you?"

Jack came right out with it—as he had no filter, or a way of saying things nice and neat—as he said, "We came to talk to you about your brother, Marcus."

Katherine looked at the boy as she had just heard a name she never wanted to hear again, but instead of saying the words *get out*, she told them to come in. She was well aware Marcus was nowhere around; so, she was safe for now. Jack and the others sat in the living room as Katherine stood up looking at them and said, "So, what do you want to know about Marcus?"

Jack spoke first as he said, "How come no one talks about him around here? I mean, what could he have possibly done to have the whole town forget him?"

Katherine poured herself some tea from a teapot that was sitting on the coffee table in front of the kids, as she sipped from the cup and said, "Well, it's the other way around. You see, no one could stop thinking about him after they found out he went on a killing spree with sharp razor knifes, and the dark, powerful magic spells he used for evil deeds to kill and murder people." Katherine imagined like it happened just yesterday as she was still talking to the kids, "Our parents were killed by my brother Marcus, as he hated our father for always hitting us and yelling at us all the time. Sometimes, he would hit us for fun just because he found it amusing, but it was not amusing for Marcus as he always protected me and my mom from him, or at least tried to.

"We all forgot about him recently because people talked about others things that were going on in their life. They would say anything just so they could forget about him and hope no one would dare find out about him. If you kids aren't careful, you could get yourselves killed. Now, what I suggest you do is, go write this down into your report and leave it be." Katherine asked nicely for the kids to leave as she was feeling quite down after talking about Marcus.

Jack looked at the others and said, "Well, guess that's all we can do for now. We can have this report done by tomorrow."

Frank looked at Jack and said, "Are you kidding?" he looked at Jack like he had three heads. "We can't go in with just that; we will definitely get an *F* on our grade, or at least a *D*."

Jack looked at Frank with a look; saying, "And what do you suppose we do, Frank?"

Frank responded with, "I say we check this guy Marcus out more and see what kind of magic he's been using. Who knows, we might find some interesting things about the spells he uses? Because it might be good for the report." The other kids agreed with Frank and thought some more info would be useful for their project. The kids went off back to Shadow Lake to see if anything was there that could have the least bit connection to Marcus Slayer, and the magic he used to cause so much chaos during his killing spree. The kids came across the Shadow Lake library, where they would, for sure, find something that had at least a knowing about the magic Marcus used all those years ago. The kids looked from top to bottom, searching all around the entire library, hoping to find something. But of course, luck would not be on their side today; or would it? As a librarian came out from behind the backroom and approached the kids. The lady who approached the kids asked the kids: "What are you looking for? 'Cause I see you looked through my entire store and haven't found anything that you like. Is there anything you kids were hoping to find in the library today?"

Jack walked towards the woman and said, "What's your name? If you don't mind me asking."

"Janet is my name; and what might your name be, young man?"

Jack looked back at the librarian and said, "My name is Jack." Jack looked at the librarian as he thought the lady could help them find a book that could link them to Marcus Slayer and the magic he was using. He said, "Hey. We're doing a project on Mar..." before he could finish saying the word *Marcus*, Jennifer nudged his arm, as she gave him a look; having Jack retract his words. "We're doing a project on magic and the different types there are in the world." The librarian knew just the book the kids were looking for, and went in the backroom to get it. As the kids were waiting, Selena saw a shadow outside of the library as though someone was sneaking around. Selena was trying to make out the shadow and see who it was but could not get a good look through the dusty old windows of the library.

The librarian returned with a book in her hand with a title called *Origins of Magic*. Janet, the librarian, said, "Well here you go kids. It's yours. Go ahead, knock yourselves out." Jack took the book as they went to a table in the library, sat down, and started to flip through the pages to see if they could find anything about evil spells.

The kids kept looking until they came across page 66. On the 6<sup>th</sup> paragraph, they saw that there was a book containing many evil and wicked spells, known to the world as *Dark Power*. This book would only appear to those who could control the power of it or those who were in need of this book to help them get revenge.

Jack and others were reading and wondering how Marcus came across this book; and then Jack put two and two together. Jack whispered to the others saying, "He must have really wanted his father dead, which is probably how he was able to get a hold of the book."

Roland thought for a second and said, "Guess he really wanted revenge 'cause he got a hold of that book; but where is it now?"

The others kids looked at each other and then looked at Roland. To which, Jack said, "What do you mean Marcus must still have it?"

Roland replied with, "Well if he had it, why isn't he causing any mayhem or chaos with his spells? Or furthermore, why isn't he killing anyone? But I think the most important question must be: What happened to him that made him stop?" Jack and others were now very curious about Marcus, for there seems to be a missing part of the whole story on how he stopped killing everyone.

A man approached the table as he knew exactly what they were doing. The man started to talk, saying, "I see you're interested in Marcus. I know my wife does not like to talk about him much."

The kids looked at the man and said, "Who are you? And how do you know Marcus?"

"Well, you see, my name is Thomas Mayfield, and I'm Katherine's husband, and since I'm sure you've talked to my wife and did not listen, might as well tell you kids a story." Jack and the others were listening as Selena looked by the window again to see if someone was still lurking outside but she did not see a shadow.

Thomas told the story to the kids saying, "So you wanna know how Marcus stopped killing, do you? Well, I will tell you but after this, you must promise to let this go and finish your report. Because I'm warning you, pursuing Marcus will only end up in disaster and will probably cost you your lives. Understand?" The kids shook their head *yes*; but only to hear the story, as they would not heed his warning. Thomas starts the story with, "It happened while he was young and still going on a rampage, until his sister Katherine stopped him.

"Katherine took the book titled *Dark Power* out of Marcus' hands while he wasn't looking, and told Marcus to stop; otherwise she was going to kill herself in front of Marcus. Marcus could never let that happen as he loved his sister way too much. Marcus told his sister, 'You win this time sister. I'll stop for now, but the second I get a hold of that book again, and you know I will, you can bet on me killing again in a heartbeat.' Marcus laughed so evil, it sent horrible chilling sensations down his sister's spine, and it gives her nightmares till this day. Katherine also took his gloves away from him, as she knew without them, Marcus could not harm another soul on Earth." Thomas had a very sad look on his face and then he looked worried as he said, "I hope Katherine hid those items well but I'm not sure what happened to the pages to Marcus' book. Katherine never told me what she did with them." Thomas ended his story as he did not know anything else than what Katherine had told him already.

Kelly spoke to Thomas saying, "Well, thank you for everything, Thomas, it was nice meeting you."

Thomas replied with, "It was nice meeting all of you kids as well. Good luck with your project."

Jack went outside as the other kids followed closely behind him, as Calvin said, "Well, that was good stuff for the report."

"Well I don't know about you guys, but I think we need more then what we got so far," said Judy.

All of a sudden Frank got an idea as though someone lit a match in a gas filled room, and it came to him like an explosion. "Why don't we try to find these pages ourselves? I mean, there has to be something we can do," said Frank.

Selena and Bobby looked at Frank saying, "Hey, that's not a bad idea, right Jack?"

Jack was quiet for a moment as he was trying to think of a way on how to get Katherine to talk to him again, as he really wants to know where those pages are. Selena called Jack's name again and this time, Jack turned around and said, "Yeah, it's not a bad idea but where do we start?"

"Well, we can try looking up any newspaper clippings on the computer to my house. I'll see if I can look it up from there," said Jennifer.

"Well that sounds like a plan, so let's head to your house."

Jennifer said, "Jack."

The kids got in their cars and started to drive over to Jennifer's house. But no one knew that the librarian had gone missing around the time Thomas Mayfield told his story to the kids. As Jack was driving his car, he once again thought about other ways he could get Katherine to talk to him again; as he was sure she knew where the pages were at. They arrived at Jennifer's house no more than twenty minutes after leaving the library. Jack parked his car as Selena and Roland parked their cars next to Jack's car. They got out of their cars as they headed inside Jennifer's house, where the group of kids got thirsty at this point; so, they all grabbed a drink from Jennifer's fridge. Afterwards, they all headed upstairs to Jennifer's room to go on her computer. Jennifer logged on her computer and as she was signing in, Jennifer happened to mention her past to the rest of the gang. "I'm really good at hacking stuff, that's why I can look up the info we need," said Jennifer. "Though, it kind of reminds me of the time I got someone in trouble because I used my neighbors name to hack into a bank account to transfer some money."

Sandy looked at Jennifer saying, "That's messed up, Jennifer, I did not know you could do something like that."

Jennifer replied with, "Eh, that neighbor had it coming. She had my car towed away for no reason once, so I thought payback was in order." Jennifer's computer was finally up and running, as it has had time to warm up by now. Jennifer immediately went onto the internet as she was looking for newspaper clippings over the past 20 years, hoping to find something on Marcus Slayer. Jennifer found a newspaper clipping titled: *Clawed kid goes on murderous rampage.* She also found another one titled

*Murderous Merlin kills dozens*. The kids read the articles on Marcus as a kid; seeing that he caused a lot of chaos and mayhem though out the town of Clouds-dale, as he had caused fires, explosions, and even killed many people with his clawed gloves.

Judy then said, "Well, this should be plenty on Marcus Slayer, so I really don't see no reason to find the pages of his spell book anymore."

Selena disagreed saying, "Well, I think we would get a definite *A+* if we were to get at least one page of the book."

The other kids besides Judy shook their heads *yes* as Jack said, "Well it would be some proof that the book existed."

Calvin said, "Well, hold on now," as Calvin and everyone paused for a second. "Maybe we oughta listen to the Mayfields. What if we are putting our lives in danger by searching for these pages?" said Calvin.

Bobby turned to Calvin and said, "Come on man, don't be such a wimp. We are all going to look for them together, so what are you so scared of?"

Calvin looked at Bobby; then the others, saying, "Maybe your right; there's nothing to worry about. Come on, let's try to find the pages. But what if Thomas was right, and they should have stayed away because something is following them."

A dark shadow follows the kids; it has been following them since the library. Jack and the others went to go look for the pages to the book titled *Dark Power.* Jennifer thought for a second and said, "Maybe Katherine does have the pages to the *Dark Power* book."

Jack looked at Jennifer and said, "Maybe you're right. I mean, she probably tricked us into thinking she didn't have the pages because she actually has them."

Kelly thought that to herself and said, "Yeah, that would make sense if she wanted to throw us, off course, and end our search."

Jack said, "Well I guess that settles it; we are going back to Katherine's house. But its only 6:00 pm right now, so we should be at her house by 6:15 pm. So, let's get going."

The gang raced off into their cars as they headed towards Katherine's house. Katherine was cooking dinner at the time, as her husband walked through the front door no more than 5 seconds after she put the ham with grilled pineapple in the oven. Thomas shouted, "Honey! I'm home, and boy does something smell good or what?"

Thomas walked in the kitchen, as he saw Katherine cooking dinner; as Katherine turned around and said, "Hey baby, it's nice to see you home." Katherine continued cooking as Thomas went upstairs to get changed into more relaxing clothes. Katherine had finished cooking the string beans for dinner, when she heard her doorbell ring. Katherine hears her husband say, "Honey, can you get that I'm kind of under dressed at the moment!"

Katherine heard Thomas from upstairs as she walked to the door saying, "It's alright, honey, I got it!" Katherine looked through the door-hole and saw the kids that were at her house earlier that day. Katherine wanted to just tell them to go away but for some reason she didn't and ended up opening the door for them as she respond with, "Oh hey kids; back again I see?

Jack looked at Katherine and said, "Yes, Mrs. Mayfield, we are, and we would love it if you could let us talk to you one more time, and then we can leave you alone for good."

Katherine looked at Jack and said, "No you won't actually, 'cause you're going to keep asking me and asking me about those pages, aren't you?"

"Yes, Katherine, we were; but please, it would help our report so much."

Katherine was turning red as she was getting mad now. She said, "The only thing you're going to do is turn around and go home and write whatever you found on my brother, and that's it; end of story, got it? Next time you come here, you better have a good reason than that coming here, 'cause if you don't and ask about my brother again, I will call the cops, got it?"

All the kids said, "Got it," as they turned around and walked away thinking that could have gone better.

Jennifer looked at Bobby, as well as Frank and Jack saying, "Well guys, got anymore useless ideas?" as she went off walking back to Jack's, feeling upset. Jack thinks for a second and comes up with another idea, *one I'm sure Jennifer won't like to hear, but it's worth a try.*

Jack runs to the car as he stops Jennifer from getting in his car. "Jennifer wait, I have another idea. Okay? So please, hear me out," Jack said, as Jennifer gives him a minute to say his idea. "Okay, so we go back to the library and look at one of the magic spell books there and see if any spells can help us find the pages," said Jack.

Jennifer, rather, found the idea intriguing and said, "You know what? I'm down for that actually."

Sandy walked over with the other guys as she said, "So, where we headed to next, fearless leader?"

Jack said, "Back to the library. We are going to do a little magic of our own."Jack and others went into their cars, as they headed back to the library unaware as to what has happened while they were away.

Meanwhile, Thomas was just getting a second helping of dinner when he brought up the kids in a conversation with Katherine, "Honey, I think you were a little hard on the kids. I mean, it's not every day we get visitors."

Katherine looked at Thomas while she was eating saying, "True, we don't get many visitors; but we can thank my brother for that."

Thomas replied with, "Katherine. Sweetie. They were just trying to get a good grade. You could have showed them a spell and then they would have left you alone that's all."

Katherine thought to herself as she said, "You're right, babe, 'cause if they keep looking for the pages, they're going to end up getting themselves killed." Katherine put her hands over her mouth saying, "Oh god, what have I done? I better find them."

Thomas said, "Okay, then I'm coming with you because when it has to do with your brother, I wanna make sure nothing happens to you."

Katherine was now worried she might have sent the college kids to their grave as she rushed to their car with her husband getting into the passenger side. Katherine had no time for road rules as she quickly drove out of her driveway and onto the street. Meanwhile, the kids had arrived at the library as it was now 6:40 pm and the library was still open. So, the kids entered to see if they could find the librarian; she could show them to where the section is on magical spell books. Jack entered the main library and thought it was too quiet, even for a library, as he looked around and didn't hear one word or whisper, or even the sound of the wind for that matter. Jack looked around closely and turned to his friends and said, "Hey guys," whispered silently. "Something doesn't feel right, I think we should split up and take a look around and see if we can find the librarian, and the books we're after."

The gang agreed as they started to split up and see just what exactly was going on. Some of the kids started to get a little scared as there was no sound what so ever; just the footsteps of the other kids walking around in the library. Calvin was looking for the librarian and so he figured he would look in the area where they last saw her. Calvin walked to the front desk, and he approached the desk; he did not see anything yet, but continued on towards the back to see if she was there. Calvin then saw a trail of blood starting from her office door and leading towards the back more. Calvin said to himself, "Holy shit, the librarian is dead." Calvin did not bother going back any further and quickly ran out of the back room only to return to the main library room. Calvin was now very scared about pursuing Marcus, as he now believed that he killed the librarian.

Kelly and Roland went looking for the librarian as well, but went more towards the basement part of the library. As Roland and Kelly made it down into the basement, they saw a double, red-metal door that had rust on it. Roland saw a sign above the double, red-metal door that said *The Staff Lounge.* Roland and Kelly thought that this was where they might find the librarian at that time—they preceded to enter the double, red doors and saw a few shelves filled with books. They also saw coffee tables along with chairs and a counter with coffee and hot chocolate packets and a hot water pitcher. Kelly said, "Well, for the most part, this room seems pretty normal; besides, I don't see the librarian anywhere in here."

Roland agreed, saying, "Yeah, I don't see her in here, maybe she's upstairs somewhere; or maybe, she still down here." Roland thought that they should look in the basement more. But the fact that there was no sound at all going through the halls of the basement kinda scared Roland and Kelly a bit; but they pressed on hoping to find the librarian. Selena was with Jack as they were looking for the area of book that had magical spells inside them. Jack saw a shelf of books with special writing on them with language he'd never seen before.

Selena saw this as well and said, "Hey, these must be the spell books the librarian was mentioning earlier." Jack and Selena immediately started to look through the book without telling the gang first. Meanwhile, Judy and Frank, as well as Jennifer and Bobby, the four of them, could not find anything as far as the librarian or the spell book were concerned.

Calvin managed to find them and as he did, he ran to them whispering loudly, "Hey guys!"

Frank and the other heard him as they turned around and saw Calvin running at them, as he thought he had just seen a ghost. Calvin stopped when he got to Frank and the others; now trying to catch his breath. Judy was worried as she said, "You okay, Calvin? You look like someone scarred the shit out of you."

Calvin caught his breath, as he said, whispering, "Dude, guys, I think the librarian has been murdered."

The four kids widened their eyes in surprise as Jennifer said, "What? How?"

Calvin replied with, "I don't know and I don't plan to find out. I mean, Thomas warned us of this, and now a woman is dead. I don't know about you guys, but I'm out." He went back to the main library to wait for them, as he did not want to search for anything or anyone anymore.

Roland and Kelly went down the basement hallway more, as they came across four doors. There were two on the left of them and two on the right of them. Roland said, "Let's look inside each door together, okay? 'Cause leaving each other alone might be a bad idea."

Kelly shook her head *yes* and said, "Okay, Roland, let's check out the left doors first." Roland agreed as they walked over to the first door together, hoping to find the librarian. Roland went first, as he opened the first door on the left, and saw a room with chairs set up in a circle as he saw a sign that said *Book Club Room.* Kelly took a peek inside as well and saw nothing but chairs and a nice, neat, organized room. Roland closed the door as he knew the librarian was nowhere to be found inside that room. Kelly and Roland went to the next room on the left to see what was in there. Roland opened up the second door on the left and noticed that the room was a classroom; but for reading. Part of this library was also a school to teach kids how to read. Roland walked in slowly and looked around as Kelly followed behind him hoping to find the librarian. But of course, they were unaware that Calvin had found the librarian dead in the back.

Behind her desk. Roland had spotted a window in the room that was opened and walked to the window only to see if anyone came in. Kelly saw Roland walk over and said, "Well did you find anything Roland?"

Roland looked carefully and saw footprints just below the window as though someone broke in. Roland looked at Kelly and said, "I think someone broke in here and wiped their feet on the carpet next to the window landing."

Kelly then looked at Roland with surprised eyes saying, "You don't think someone killed the librarian, do you?"

Roland, now with a worried look, said, "It's possible. We were gone for a short time; long enough for someone to surely do the job." Roland looks around and says, "But that still leaves the question unanswered."

Kelly then says, "Where's the librarian?" as Roland and Kelly head out of the room; only to now check the other two room across from them. Just as Roland and Kelly started to walk to the rooms, Frank came down the stairs, startling both Roland and Kelly; as Frank said, "Hey guys!"

Roland and Kelly were glad to see Frank and said, "What's up, Frank? You find something?"

Frank replied with, "Yeah, the corpse of the librarian, so I think it's safe to say we found her."

Roland and Kelly joined the others upstairs without checking the last two doors on the right. As the kids headed upstairs, a shadowy figure looked through one of the door windows on the right side and smiled as he saw them. Frank, Roland and Kelly meet up with Bobby, Judy, and Jennifer in the main library. Sandy appeared out of nowhere as Frank whispered, "Where have you been?"

Sandy said, "Sorry, I saw a good book and started reading it; guess I lost track of time. Why? What's going on?"

After Frank got done explaining the situation to Sandy, Jack and Selena showed up saying, "I think we found our spell book guys."

As Jack walked in, he said, "Hey where's Calvin?"

Frank said, "Well he left to wait outside in the car because he found the librarian dead."

Jack said, "Oh shit, really? What happened?"

"Calvin believes she was murdered; but by who, we don't know," said Jennifer.

Selena went behind the desk to look at the body of Janet, the librarian. Selena looked at the body and saw that the librarian's chest was cut wide open as she noticed a trail of blood from her body to the wall. Selena looked up at the wall and saw the librarians heart nailed to the wall. As she saw that, she was scared to go on and went back in the main library with the rest of the crew. Jack entered the back room to find a note on the table as Jack picked it up and read it saying, *"Knowledge is power*; too bad 'cause she didn't know a damn thing," he chuckled.

Jack knew this might be Marcus' work; and he might have been the one that killed her. Jack walked out of the room with the note in his hands as he thought to himself about what the note could mean. Jennifer and the others saw Jack walk out of the backroom unharmed as he was holding a note in his hands. Bobby said, "Hey what's that note say?" As Jack walked over to the counter of the desk and laid it down for everyone to read.

Selena read the note and said, "What does this note mean Jack? Because I'm confused."

Katherine and Thomas appeared behind them and startled the kids by saying, "It means he's looking for his pages and his claw gloves."

Katherine was glad to see none of the kids were hurt but her face went from relief to sad as she walked over to the desk and saw blood on the ground. She said, "Oh my goodness, what happened?"

Jack said, with a glum look on his face, "Marcus killed the librarian."

Katherine had a scared look in her eyes as she knew Marcus was strong enough to get out again. Judy looked at Katherine and said, "What do u mean strong enough? You mean he wasn't always this strong?"

Katherine said, "No, because I drained him of his physical strength and took the pages out of his book, so he could do no more harm. This was so many years ago that I guess he found a way to get his strength back."

Thomas looked at the kids and said, "Look, we told you kids to stay out of this and just write your little report and get a grade."

Katherine said, "Well it looks like you will find the pages eventually, so here you go." Katherine gives the kids a page from the *Dark Power* book, and the page had three spells on the front and three on the back. The kids wrote down the spells in their note books as they wanted to make sure they didn't forget this information. "Just remember that I'm giving you this page for your report only," said

Katherine. Katherine gets Jack's information just in case they forget to bring it back. Katherine looks at the kids and says, "I hope you all will be safe tonight."

Jack and the others replied with, "Yeah, we will. Thank you, Mrs. Mayfield."

Jack and the others start walking out of the library as Frank stops and called the cops to inform them of the dead librarian. Jack stopped Frank as he said, "Hold on, let someone else find her."

"I'm sure someone will find her just where she is."

Roland said, "Why man? She's dead she needs to be in a morgue. We can't just leave her in there."

Jack says, "Well, if the cops come, they're going to want to know who did it; and if word gets out that its Marcus again, I'm sure this town will be in the shit and go nuts."

# Chapter 2
## A Book Full of Intentions

Sandy and Kelly agree and say, "You know what? Jack has a point; the less people know…the better."

Calvin walked with the group to the cars as he was worried about Marcus killing him and his friends. Jennifer looks at Calvin as she slows down to talk to him in the back of the group. "What's on your mind, Calvin?" said Jennifer.

"Well I'm just worried that we're going to die," said Calvin. "'Cause I think Marcus is after these pages, and if he finds out we have them, he might try to kill us."

Jennifer says, "Well let's just get home to my house and right this report 'cause this night has been way too hectic for one little story. So after today, we're done with this story; so, don't worry about Marcus killing us." Calvin had a slight sense of relief; just enough to get him through the night.

They all returned to Jennifer's house to start writing the report, so they all sat up in Jennifer's room and wrote down all the info they learned about Marcus. Jack was looking at the page as he was writing, when he thought to himself, *hmm, wonder if one of these spells could be useful.*

One of the many spells that caught Jacks eye was the location spell. The location spell was a spell that allowed the user to find any object that they were seeking; or to place a small ball of light onto a person or object, so they could never lose them. Jack wanted to try it out as it seemed like a harmless spell, but of course, leave that thinking to a college idiot of a kid. Jack tried to chant the words softly as he was trying to activate the spell. All of a sudden Selena, Frank, and Roland catch Jack chanting a spell from the page they received. They busted in the room to pull the page out of Jacks hand without ripping it. "You must be a new kind of stupid if you really think we're going to start chanting these spells now," yelled Roland.

"Jack, what the hell were you thinking?" said Frank and Selena.

Jack just gave a look, saying, "What it's just a harmless spell." The others came in when they heard Roland yell; as Selena explained why he yelled.

Jennifer says, "Are you insane, Jack? Look, I know we all want a good grade and…"

Before Jennifer could Finish Jack cut her off. Jack says, "Well, then lets at least do one spell, and see how this magic works; 'cause the detail for this report will guarantee us a sure-fire $A++$."

Calvin walked away and sat in Jennifer's room as he started to dose off. Having it be only 7:15 pm, he seemed tired after today with the dead librarian and all. Calvin was now dreaming but he dreamed that he was at school, in class, laughing with his friends about boy stuff, when a teacher appeared, one that he never saw before. Calvin looked closely at the teacher but could not recognize him from anywhere. The teacher in his dream spoke, saying, "Now, class, behave or I'll have to kill you." The classroom started to chuckle from the teacher's playful threat but Calvin did not laugh as a smile was wiped from his face. In Calvin's dream, Jack shoots a spit ball at the teacher as he was writing on the chalkboard. Calvin says, "What are you doing? You're going to piss him off."

"What are you worried about?"

Jack said, "Calvin, he's just a teacher." The teacher felt the spit ball hit the back of his neck and when he did, he turned around to look directly at Jack. The teacher says, "You shouldn't have done that, Jack, 'cause now I have to teach you a lesson you won't forget." The teacher in Calvin's dream took his index finger and moved it horizontal under Jack's head. Jack's head came clean off his body as blood started to squirt and fountain out of his body as it fell out of the chair. Calvin started to scream and yell for help while the other classmates started laughing and having fun in the puddle of blood that came from Jack's corpse.

No more than a few seconds after that happened Sandy and Judy woke up Calvin, saying, "Are you okay, Calvin? You look like you saw a ghost."

Calvin says, "I don't know what I saw, but I'm not feeling safe with this whole spell report thing."

Sandy says, "Don't worry, no one's going to perform a spell from the book, okay?"

Judy followed Sandy's words saying, "Yeah, we're going to make sure we finish this report without drama." Bobby makes sure the page of spells is with him and Jennifer; as they were keeping it away from Jack. The group continued to write down all the information they could about the events that took place today after school. Meanwhile, in the dream that Calvin had, the teacher was still there as he walked around the classroom as though it was frozen in time. The teacher then turned into Marcus Slayer as he started to laugh saying, "I'm sure whoever these kids are, they can help me find what I'm looking for." Marcus muttered to himself, "I know I'm not that strong here in the dream realm, but I think I remember a spell that can help me get those kids to do my biding." Marcus awoke from his dream spell that he chanted on himself only to find him back in the basement of the library. Marcus got up and walked out the room as he was strolling through the halls on his way towards the exit to leave the library. Marcus thought to himself, *If I only took the time to remember some of the other spells, I could have gotten my gloves back by now as well as my pages for my book.* " Marcus took out the cover of the book called *Dark Power* from his bag that he carried around.

Marcus was chanting the spells he remembered in his head so that they would not be activated, and draw attention to himself. Marcus knew a total of three spells at the moment, and one of the spells he knew was dream realm, which allowed the user to go into a sleep state and go into anyone's dreams as long as they are asleep, but not touch or feel anything while in the realm. The second spell was called dream skin. This spell allowed the user to feel and interact with another person's dream. The third spell was called dream power, this spell gave the user the ability to commit supernatural feats such as psychic abilities or alternating the reality of the persons dreams. The second and third spell could not be chanted in real life for they didn't work while you were in the real world. Marcus always had to chant the dream realm spell first before chanting the second and third spell. When Marcus chanted these spells in the dream realm, they worked and stayed activated until the user woke up or left the dream realm for any reason. Marcus walks to a nearby graveyard as he approaches a tombstone saying, *Here lies the Syler family.* Marcus presses something on the tombstone and a sliding door moves in front of the grave, as it shows a staircase leading to an underground hideout. Marcus walks down the stairs as he reaches his hideout and relaxes; as he thinks of a plan on how he will get the kids to do his bidding for him. Back at Jennifer's house, they all wrote down as much as they could to finish their report. Jennifer took everyone's reports and combined it into one story and as she was typing, she started to get tired. Frank looked at the time and saw it was 11:30 pm, and it was at this time, Frank said, "Well, I think we should hit the hay, it's getting late." Jack and the others agreed with Frank as it was late and they did need sleep, so they decided to sleep over in Jennifer's spare room; where the guys slept. The girls slept in Jennifer's room as they all got ready for a good night sleep, except Calvin as he was too wide awake to even bother sleeping. Calvin was still thinking about that dream and the teacher that was in it. Calvin was scared to go back to sleep as he thought he was going to see the teacher again.

Calvin was wondering that if he does go back into his dream maybe the teacher wouldn't be there anymore, maybe it was only a one-time thing. Calvin kept worrying and worrying and soon enough, he worried himself to sleep as it was now 11:50 pm. Calvin was now dreaming as he was wondering the halls of his college inside the building where his dorm was. Calvin was just walking as he was looking around for the teacher to see if he was anywhere to be found, until he bumped into Selena and Jennifer in the dream.

Jennifer says, "Hey, Calvin, the dean wants to see you in his office"

Selena follows with, "Yeah, I hope you're not in trouble or anything."

Calvin starts walking to the dean's office as he notices the hallway begin to stretch as it seems to be getting longer and longer, like it would take forever to get to the dean's office. Calvin then heard a wicked laugh in the hallway as he was walking and got a little scared. Calvin got closer to the dean's office and as he got closer and closer, the dean's door got bigger and bigger. Calvin was afraid of going in until he heard Jack and Bobby behind him. Jack says, "Hey, Calvin, you headed to the dean's office too huh?"

Calvin looked at Jack and said, "Yeah, why? You guys were headed to the dean's office too?" They opened the door to the dean's office as they saw three chairs in the room. Jack and Bobby took the seats on the right and left of Calvin as Calvin goes to sit in the middle chair. Calvin sits quietly until the dean of the college starts to speak. "So, you boys have been causing trouble in my school again huh?" said the dean.

To which, Calvin began to say, "Sir we haven't been doing anything wrong."

The dean turns around in his chair and it was at this point, Calvin definitely was scared as he saw the teacher from his last dream sitting in dean's chair. Calvin said with a shiver in his voice, "Wh…wha…what do you want from me?"

The teacher, all of a sudden, turns into the one and only Marcus Slayer, as he introduces himself to the boy. "Hello there, kiddo," he laughs in a creep-like chuckle. "My name is Marcus Slayer. I don't know how you kids know so much about me, but guess what? I know where you are and know where you live now." Calvin kept getting more afraid by the second. "So, guess what? I'm going to tell you a secret. That secret is…well there is a spell in one of my pages from the book that can defeat me forever which means I'll never come back. So, sport, you up for a page hunt?" laughs more as Calvin looks to Jack, and sees him headless and gushing blood. Calvin then looks to Bobby with his eyes completely red, bleeding out a stream of blood from both eyes.

It was at this moment Calvin woke up screaming, saying, "Oh shit, he's going to kill us," as he ran down out the spare bedroom. He ran into the living room as he grabbed hold of a pillow and gripped it tight as he could not stop thinking about what he just saw in the dream. Jack and the other guys woke up as they went to chase down Calvin into the living room. Jack and the others arrived in the living room, as they saw Calvin afraid for his life as though someone had tried to kill him.

Jack went to Calvin saying, "Dude, what's wrong? You look like you've seen a ghost or something."

Calvin looked at Jack saying, "I saw him Jack…I saw Marcus Slayer."

Jack said, "What? Are you serious?"

Bobby was interested, saying, "So what was he like?" while Frank and Roland stand next to Calvin and try to help him up.

Calvin looks at Jack and goes, "Yes, I really did meet him." And then he looked at Bobby saying, "He scared me, and he knows where we live," he said.

Jack and the other guys said, "What? What else did he say?"

Calvin continued saying, "He says if we want to stop him, we have to look for the pages of the book, 'cause he said there is a spell in the book that can defeat him so that he never comes back again."

Roland looked at Calvin saying, "Are you for real man? There ain't no way for someone to contact you in your dreams and say all this to you. I mean, you've never seen the guy before. Look I'm sure this was all just a nightmare, and you will feel better after some breakfast, so let's get some sleep and wake up in a few hours, okay? 'Cause it's 4:30 am." So, the guys all went back to bed including Calvin even after he had encountered Marcus twice now. Through the rest of the night, Calvin didn't have any more nightmares. In fact, Calvin slept pretty well the rest of the night; as everyone woke up around 8:00 am to get up shower and have breakfast.

Jennifer and the girls were in Jennifer's room combing their hair as they had taken their showers already. Jack and Bobby were setting up the table for breakfast as Frank and Selena cooked the breakfast. Sandy comes walking out of

Jennifer's room and into the kitchen as she smells the good food Frank and Selena are cooking. Sandy breathes in the scent of the food as she says with a nice morning sigh, "Oh man, that smells good what are you cooking, guys? It smells great."

Frank replied with, "Bacon and scrambled eggs with cheese, along with some pork roll."

Selena looks at Sandy and says, "Yeah and I'm making stuffed French toast."

After all the kids finished getting ready, everyone was sitting at the table eating breakfast except Calvin; but no one had noticed that he wasn't even at the table. Jack was eating when he brought it up, saying, "Calvin had a bad nightmare last night."

Kelly said, "Really? What happened?"

He said, "Marcus Slayer found him in his dreams and told him to look for the pages of the book."

Selena says, "Why even bother? All we have to do is hand in our report and get a good grade, okay? So, let's just do that."

Sandy says, "Well why would he tell him to look for the pages? It doesn't make any sense to haunt someone for that."

"That's what I said 'cause I think he's crazy; the dude is tired and is obviously in need of some therapy," said Roland.

Jennifer looks around and now notices Calvin is not with them at the table so she looks to Jack and says, "Jack, where's Calvin at?"

Jack says, "I guess he never got up, so I'll go wake him up and tell him breakfast is ready." Jack walked back to the spare room as Calvin was in a chair with a blanket over his body as he was sleeping. Jack, at least, thought he was sleeping, until he went to go wake him up. Jack put his hand on Calvin's shoulder, and said, "Come on, man, rise and shine." It was at this moment Calvin's head flew back half way like a PEZ dispenser with his eyes missing from his body. Jack saw this as his body jumped back to the wall and screaming, "Oh man, what the fuck!"

The crew ran from the table as Jack screamed and saw Calvin's body there in the chair with his head half-cut and eyes missing; they were horrified by what had happened to Calvin. Jennifer and the other girls started to cry; as Kelly—really liked Calvin a lot—was hoping to go to the college dance with him. The guys stood in shock as they still couldn't get over the fact that Calvin was dead. Jack realized at this point that Calvin was telling the truth about his nightmare. Jack looks towards the others as he says, "Guys, calm down and keep it together."

As Jennifer looks at him screaming. "Are you kidding me, Jack? Calvin is dead for God's sake. What even happened; that nightmare you were talking about?" said Jennifer.

Jack looks at Jennifer saying, "Calvin said Marcus told him to find the pages to the book 'cause he said there is a spell that can kill him."

"We have to go see that Katherine girl again," said Frank, "but before that they call the police on the events that happened."

The girls mourned the loss of their friend Calvin, as the guys just sat and waited for the police to arrive. Frank was on the phone now, calling them and telling the police what happened. Jack looks at the page of spells they received from Katherine, and tried to find a spell that could bring Calvin back to life; but no such spell was on that piece of paper. Besides the location spell, Jack only found seven other spells on that piece of paper; all of them were harmful. Jack didn't want to push his luck so he just waited like everyone else for the police to arrive. The police arrived on the scene; came through the front door with two officers with flashlights as they saw Jack.

Jack says, "This way, officers, our friend is in here," as the officers entered the room with the kids in the living room, still crying and sad over the loss of their friend. One officer looks at the body of Calvin and the other officer checks on the others kids.

The one officer is with Jack as the officer looks at the body and says, "Good god, I haven't seen a body like this since…"

Before the officer could finish Jack looks at the officer's name tag and says, "So, Officer Humble, would you like my statement?"

Officer Humble says, "Uh yeah, I would, but let's sit in the kitchen and do it."

The other officer checks on the kids, saying, "Okay kids, my name's Officer Gerald and I would like to know what happened here tonight."

Jennifer blows her nose as she continues to cry saying, "I'm sorry sir, I wouldn't know; I didn't see what happened."

Roland looked at the officer and says, "I know what happened, sir," as he gets nervous as he is about to tell him the truth.

Officer Gerald says, "Okay, what happened?"

Roland replied with, "We believe he was killed by Marcus Slayer, sir, and that he killed him in his dreams."

Officer Gerald says, "Look, that's not a funny prank, kids, okay? 'Cause Marcus Slayer is long since gone; so, someone better tell me the truth, or you're all going downtown."

Jack gave his statement as it was the same as the one Roland gave. So, the officers didn't believe them as they were all brought down to the station in four police cars. The ten kids all shared the same jail cell until the officer would come back and find out who killed that young boy Calvin. The kids waited for about ten minutes until an officer unlocked their jail cell finding out they have been not only been released but found innocent of all charges.

The kids went out front to the police station lobby only to find Katherine and her husband Thomas waiting there for them. Katherine said, "Oh my. Are you kids okay? I heard what happened."

Jack looks at Katherine saying, "We need your help."

Katherine looks at Jack as she replies with, "I know you do, and now I'm willing to help. I didn't think he would find you; I don't know how he did in the first place you were completely safe unless…"

Frank looks at Katherine and says, "Unless what?"

Katherine says, "Unless you chanted a spell from the page I gave you."

Everyone at that moment looked at Jack as Jennifer went up to Jack and slapped him so hard that his head went sideways. "You bastard, it's because of you Calvin's dead," as she starts to cry again.

Katherine looks at Jack saying, "What spell did you say, Jack?"

Jack says, "The location spell, I thought it would be cool to try it out. I didn't know he would find us."

Kelly and Sandy get up to talk to Katherine and say, "We knew something was wrong 'cause Calvin had a day-mare before he went to sleep."

Katherine said, "What day-mare? What was it about?"

"It was about a teacher killing Jack in the middle of class right in front of Calvin," said Kelly.

Katherine says, "Yup, sounds like my brother alright; guess it's time to use the spells now. If we don't, Marcus will kill us the next time we go to sleep 'cause long as he knows where we are, he can get into our dreams."

Jack says, "And he knows where we are as long as we cast or chant a spell huh?"

Katherine replies with, "Yup that's right."

Katherine looks at Thomas and says, "Get the car started, it's time to go back to the library."

The kids then and there were stunned to hear those words. Could it be that the pages were there the whole time? All the kids got dressed and drove to the library as it was now 9:00 in the morning. Katherine was nervous about doing this cause she wanted to leave this part of her life behind her. Thomas, her husband, says, "Don't worry, honey, it will be over soon."

Katherine looks at Thomas and says, "It's only just begun, honey." They arrived at the library only to find cops blocking the entrance, so they get out of the car as Katherine walks up to the cop and says, "What's going on, Officer?"

The officer says, "I'm sorry, miss, but I'm afraid you can't go in there. We found the librarian's body in there on the wall; dead."

Katherine showed a face to the officer as though she was surprised and shocked, saying, "Oh my goodness, Officer. Who would do such a thing?"

The officer says, "We don't know yet, miss, but we will," as Katherine leads the kids around the back as the husband Thomas stays back with the car. Katherine knew a secret entrance in the basement back door, as she picks up a flower pot by the backdoor and finds a key. Katherine unlocks the door as she lets the kids in quietly. Jack and the others look around and find out they are in the art room in the basement. Katherine tells the kids to be quiet as she whispers, and walks ahead to lead the kids to where the pages are for Marcus' spell book. Katherine goes in to the ladies' room and turns around to say, "Okay, no ones in here, let's go," as they sneak in trying not to make a sound. Katherine walks the kids to the back wall of the ladies' room only to look at the wall and then look at the mirrors above the sinks.

Judy and Frank look at her saying, "What are you doing?"

As Roland replies with, "She's trying to find a hidden passage, right?"

Katherine looks at Roland; then looks back at the mirror and says, "Not looking…found," and so she looks in the middle mirror and chants a few words from a spell on the page they have. After the chant, a wall opens up like a door as it shows a hidden passage and a shelf with a box. Katherine takes the box as she looks at kids and says, "I remembered one spell from that page I gave you and that was the hidden spell."

Katherine opens up the box and sees that there's only half of the pages to the book in the box. Jennifer says, "Hey, where are the rest of the pages?"

Katherine says, "They are in another hidden place but first, let's look through these pages to see if we can locate a spell to get rid of Marcus Slayer once and for all."

Jack and Bobby got a few pages to look through while Jennifer and Selena looked through some pages of their own.

Frank and Judy helped out as Roland, Kelly and Sandy were sitting down and relaxing, waiting for them to get done looking through the pages. Ten minutes passed and they could find all sorts of harmful spells, but none seemed like it would stop Marcus for good. Roland looked at Katherine and said, "So, I guess this means we have to go to the other location to get the rest of the pages."

Katherine looks at Roland and says, "Yes, I believe we do, and we better hustle cause we're burning daylight." The gang gets up and goes back from where they came; carefully, to make sure they were not spotted by cops. After getting back into their cars, they turned around and headed the other way. Katherine was sitting in the passenger side as her husband drove to the next location; which would be the ancient Clouds-dale graveyard. The ancient Clouds-dale graveyard was the biggest graveyard in Clouds-dale, and nearly over fifteen-hundred people were buried there. Katherine knew where exactly to go and so, the other kids drove behind her and followed her into the graveyard. Frank looked around and said, "I'm not too fond of graveyards; they give me the creeps."

Bobby, Judy, and Selena would agree that the graveyard is not their favorite place to be. Katherine was telling Thomas where to drive to so they could get to the gravestone to where the pages are. Thomas gives Katherine a weird look, saying, "Are you sure you want to do this, honey? 'Cause I don't want you getting hurt."

Katherine looks at her husband and smiles, saying, "Don't worry, dear. I'll be fine but these kids won't be if we don't help them." They were coming close to the gravestone; as Katherine could recognize some of the gravestones, so she knew that they are going the right way. Katherine notices a tree that looked like a man holding his arms out with pom poms. They stop as Katherine tells Thomas to pull over, as she gets out of the car and starts to look for the gravestone. The kids get out of their cars as they follow Katherine, who is finding the gravestone. Selena looks around and started thinking of horrible zombie scenarios. Selena looks to Jack and says, "You know what? I'm gonna wait in the car."

Jack looks to Selena and says, "Wait, we can't split up that's just what Marcus wants." Katherine spots a gravestone from a distance and believes it could be the one they were looking for.

Katherine and the kids arrive at the gravestone and notice the headstone says *Here lies B. pages*, as Katherine says, "YES! we found it." Jack looks at the gravestone and doesn't get it at first, but looks more closely and sees *B. pages* as book pages, as it was a little clever play on words. Katherine stands in front of the gravestone as she looks around it, hoping nothing has harmed it. Kelly looks at her and says, "Wait, are you saying you buried the pages here? Are you kidding me?"

Katherine says, "Yup, we're going to be in and out in no time," as the kids look at her like she's lost it.

Frank says, "You think we are going to dig a grave to get some pages and think it will take no time at all? You've lost it, haven't you?"

Katherine looks at the kids with a clever, smart look in her eyes, saying, "Please, kids, you have to stop thinking the hard way." Katherine conjures the hidden spell once more; except this time, she was able to place her hand in the gravestone and pull out the rest of the pages. Now that they had all the pages to Marcus' book, they headed back to the car as Katherine said, "Come on, we will look at this when we get back to my place." It was getting late now as it was 5:00 pm at night as it took a long time to drive through the graveyard and back to Katherine's house.

Roland thinks in the car as they head back, hoping that all of this will seem like a bad dream and that this whole thing with Marcus is almost over. Judy looks at Roland as she tries to relax in the back saying, "What's up, Roland? You okay?"

Roland looks at Judy responding with, "Yeah, I'm fine, I just want this nightmare to end so we can get things back to normal."

Jack tells Roland, "Look, I'm sorry I got us into this mess, but don't worry this will all end as soon as we find that spell." All Jennifer could do is sit in the passenger side seat and think about Calvin as she started to doze off into a small dream.

Jennifer was dreaming, but did not know it yet, as when she opened her eyes she was still in the car. Jennifer looked around at first and everything seemed normal, as she even looked over to the left and saw Jack driving. Jennifer says to Jack, "When are we going to get there, Jack? It's getting late." Jack did not respond at first, which lead Jennifer to believe that something was wrong, as she looked around back and saw Roland, Judy, and Bobby sitting down just fine. Jennifer turned her head around to see Marcus' head on Jack's body as he says, "We're here!" shouting at her face, as he slaps her extremely hard across the face, causing her to wake up. Jennifer wakes up to Jack in front of her saying, "We're here Jennifer. Come on," as Jennifer couldn't help but slap Jack in the face.

"You bastard, why didn't you wake me up?" Jack was not aware that she had passed out; nor did Roland, or Judy, or Bobby know; they thought she was just being quiet.

Jack says, "What was that for?" as he felt his face from the slap that she gave him on his left side. "I didn't do anything to you."

Jennifer feels her face as she starts to tear a bit, saying, "I was attacked by Marcus, and I thought I was still dreaming I'm sorry," as she started to cry a bit in Jack's shirt as Jack held her.

Jack looked at her face to see where Marcus attacked her, and he only noticed a big, red mark on her face. Jack looked at Jennifer's watery eyes, saying, "He slapped you, didn't he?"

"Yes, he did, Jack," said Jennifer. "Please, we have to find that spell." The gang got to Katherine's house as Jack held Jennifer walking to her house from the car. Everyone, including Katherine and her husband, got in the house and went into the kitchen and living room to sit down and look through the pages.

Katherine noticed Jennifer was shaken up, as she asked Jack, "What happened?"

Jack says, "Marcus attacked her. Jennifer dozed off in the car, so I think it's a warning, saying to not fall asleep 'cause I'm sure Marcus could have done worse."

Everyone hears this, but Frank says, "Well, I guess we should get to looking for the spell before we get sleepy." Everyone takes a few pages a piece and looks through them thoroughly to see if any spell could get rid of Marcus once and for all.

Selena found a spell that was called magic dust. "So, let's see. Magic dust, huh? Magic dust is a powerful spell that allows the user to destroy an item and have it turn into magic dust," said Selena. "This dust can be used to make any spell five times more powerful than it is, but only works for elemental spells and healing spells," Selena continued.

Jack thought he stumbled upon it as he saw a spell called earth burial. Jack reads about it, saying, "Hmm, earth burial sounds like a good spell to kill Marcus with. Earth Burial is a spell that targets a life form or an object and drags it down into the earth itself, burying it twenty-feet deep into the ground," said Jack. This gives a small amount of space of air for the life form to breathe for a short time, and then slowly die in its burial tomb," continued Jack. Jack finishes reading the spell, saying, "And if an object gets buried, it will be crushed and lost forever in a matter of thirty minutes if not reversed in time." Katherine thought these were good spells but knew that Marcus knew how to reverse the spells, but does not remember the spells in the book; besides the dream spells. Marcus, however, was sitting in the dream realm hoping that his plan was going exactly as he had planned it. Marcus knew that they would get the pages, as he could feel it when he saw Jennifer in her own dream. Marcus clinched his fists in rage and happiness as he felt the book's power. Marcus wanted to strike but needed to know how to find a way to trick the kids into getting his gloves out and showing where they are. Marcus now awaits as he patiently keeps an eye.

Kelly looked through her pages and really couldn't find anything that could really help them defeat Marcus. Sandy looked through her pages and found a spell called dreadful tears, as it interested her more than the other spells. "The dreadful tear spell is a spell that allows the target to cry or leak blood from the targets eyes," says Sandy. "The target's body will drain of blood in a matter of minutes as the drainage flow from the person's body increases every minute," continued Sandy. Sandy though thought for a minute, and thinks that Marcus might have a way around that.

Katherine looked at Thomas and said, "I really don't know if we are going to be able to stop my brother this time."

Thomas looks at Katherine and says, "Why not? He has no power really, and you know where his gloves are. So, what could go wrong?"

Katherine then said, "I hate that line 'cause somehow, it always makes things worse."

# Chapter 3
## Hidden Intentions

Katherine stops for a second to think as she may have an idea, and that idea for the moment was kept hidden from the rest of the gang. Thomas looked at his wife Katherine and asked, "Honey, are you okay?"

"Of course, dear," said Katherine.

Roland looked at everyone for a second and then looked at Katherine and said, "Is there anything Marcus is trying to get after?"

Katherine says, "Yeah, these pages and his claw gloves, which are pretty much his killing tools for a mass murder."

Roland says, "Well, why don't we get them and burn them up so he can't use them anymore. I mean, we got to do something."

Jack agrees with Roland and says, "I think Roland is right. If we destroy his gloves; he won't have them anymore."

Selena says, "Lord knows it would take him a while to make another pair, right? So why not?"

Frank says, "Well, it would give us enough time to find a spell that could kill him, 'cause right now, we're not having any luck."

Jennifer thinks, and says, "Well, remember, he can still kill us in our dreams too, you know. So, we got to be ahead of this guy."

Katherine thinks if she really wants to go get the gloves, *because they are safe right where they are. Marcus has not found the gloves and if he did know where they were, why not get them? Why wait at all?* Katherine looks at the kids and says, "I know where the gloves are, but I don't think it's a good idea. 'Cause if he knows where they are, then were screwed."

Roland looks at Katherine, as they all do, and says, "Well, maybe you're right, but what if Marcus knows where they are? What if he's trying to find a way in now?"

Katherine replies with, "Look, he has not found the gloves yet, and I don't think he ever will. So, I really think it's best to keep the gloves right where they are."

Bobby thinks for a second as they continue to argue over the gloves to whether or not they should find them. Judy thinks the same thing; and at the same time, Bobby and Judy come up with the same idea. Bobby and Judy shouted saying, "Hey, why don't we have a vote on it? Since were having such a stubborn debate about it."

Katherine says, "No, no way. Absolutely not, will we be doing that."

Sandy says, "Look, Katherine, like it or not, Marcus is out for our blood; as much as yours probably. So, if we're going to die; we might as well get a say in this."

The husband Thomas agreed and said, "You know; there right. They already lost one of their friends."

Katherine looks at Thomas with a weird look, saying, "It's their fault for getting themselves into this. They should have known better."

Thomas looks back at Katherine with an even more sad look, saying, "Honey, I'm going to ask you a question and you better be honest." Thomas looked at the kids then back at Katherine and said, "Do they deserve to die because they didn't know better?"

Katherine looked deep into her heart before answering, because she knew she was not her brother Marcus. Katherine looks at the kids, now with a smile and a tear sliding down her cheek, as she asked them, "So you wanna take a vote?"

Jack answered back saying, "Yes, we do wanna vote to see who would want to get the gloves and who does not."

Thomas gets a piece of paper and tears it up into multiple pieces until everyone has a piece of paper. Then Thomas gives all the kids and his wife pens to write down their answers with. Thomas and everyone in the room write down and answer; and then fold up the paper and put it on the coffee table in the room. Thomas looks at everyone and asks them, "So everyone done?" as the kids and the wife shake their head *yes*.

Katherine says, "Okay, honey, would you do the honors, please?"

Thomas says, "Okay, so let's get this over with," as he picks up the first piece of paper and opens it up and says, "Okay, we go get the gloves." Thomas marks a tally mark on another piece of paper, "Forget the glove," as he picks up the next piece saying, "Don't get gloves." It finally came down to the last vote, as it was five to five and so, he picks up the last paper and says, "Get the gloves." Thomas and Katherine were a little shocked, but not really; hoping it would have been 'don't get gloves.' Jack, Jennifer, Roland, Frank, Selena, and Bobby said *yes* while Thomas, Katherine, Kelly, Judy, Sandy said *no*; but it was a fair vote.

Katherine looks at the kids and says, "Okay, you win, I'll show you where I put the gloves."

The kids shout *yes* in a very exciting tone, as they are ready to take care Marcus once and for all. Katherine and Thomas get ready, as they will need a few supplies to get through the journey. Jack and the kids wait outside as Katherine and Thomas come outside with backpacks on, ready to go. Katherine and Thomas put their backpacks in the trunk of their car as they say, "Come kids, we're all going in one car."

Jack looks at their car, and it looked like it could fit only 8 people, as he says, "Um, I don't think we are going to fit in there." Katherine pushes a button and turns the trunk section into an extra four seat section, as the bags went safe under the car in a storage place. The kids get in the car as Katherine is all set and ready to ride, as she starts the car while the everyone buckles up. Katherine takes off as she starts to drive through Clouds-dale and it seems like quite a ride. That is until they come to a street called Walk n' wall St.

Katherine turns right and stops in front of a red, brick wall and gets out of the car. The other kids had question marks above their heads, wondering what she was doing as they had nowhere else to go. Thomas gets out of the car as the kids are now curious to what could be so important about a red, brick wall. Katherine and Thomas stand in front of the brick wall in the center, as they look at each other; as they start the process to get Marcus' gloves. Katherine asks Thomas for the chalk that's located in the bag that Thomas was currently holding. Thomas hands her the chalk as she carefully draws a door-like rectangle on the wall and gives the chalk back to Thomas. The kids are confused to what is going on, but slowly start to get out of the car as their curiosity becomes stronger. Katherine knocks on the wall like a door; but not just anywhere on the wall: Only inside the rectangle that she drew. Katherine then says a few words backwards; easily, as though it was a second language to her. Katherine stands back after that and watches as the rectangle open up and slide into the brick wall itself; like a sliding door would. The kids sit there with their jaws to the ground, as they had no words to say to what just happened. Katherine and Thomas walk through the wall as the kids follow closely behind them. Everyone appears normal and safe, as they walked into a white room and although it seemed big, it was actually quite a small room. Katherine and Thomas walked to the middle of the room as though something was there but naturally, the kids saw nothing. Katherine asks her husband Thomas for the eraser and so, Thomas pulled one out of the bag and handed it to her. Katherine slowly started to erase an invisible force field with it as it showed that the gloves were behind it the whole time.

Katherine was finished with the eraser, as she put it back in the bag and said a few more words backwards, as the force field vanished and the gloves dropped in Thomas' hands. Katherine and Thomas exit back through the wall with the kids without saying a word. Roland looks at Katherine after they get through the wall, saying, "So what was all that fancy talk back there?"

Katherine looks back saying, "I had to learn a few tricks to keep ahead of Marcus. So, I learned to speak a few words backwards; so, the passwords would be harder to do."

Frank looks at Katherine and says, "Smart idea. No wonder Marcus never got the gloves; he didn't think you'd resort to magic."

Thomas looks at Frank, as he looks to all the kids saying, "Yes, we had to; it was the only way."

Marcus just then picks up a feeling; as he felt magic being used somewhere as he follows his senses through the dream world. Marcus comes to a street, in the dream world, of Clouds-dale where he feels the power of magic being used. Marcus has a feeling that the kids are here and does his dark magic, as he makes the area sleepy with his strong aura. Back in the real world, Katherine and the others start to feel a weird feeling in the air as Katherine screams, "OH SHIT! He found us. Quick, RUN!" Everyone starts running away from the area, as getting in the car would have took too long.

Jack says, as he runs and *pants*, "What are we running from?"

Katherine yells out, "Marcus is making the area sleepy. I know that smell; he did that to me a few times." While the group of kids ponder that piece of information, everyone starts to get very sleepy.

Thomas looks at Katherine saying, "Oh no, we weren't fast enough," as his voice sounds fainter by the second.

The kids feel it as well as they were not fast enough to escape Marcus' sleep aura; as they started to slow down. Katherine, strangely enough, was the only one who didn't fall asleep, as she saw her husband and the kids drift off into slumber land. Katherine was worried more about her husband more than anything else. Katherine was worried about the kids too; just not as much as her husband. Marcus now had the kids and Thomas in the dream world and was ready to have some fun. Jack looked around and saw his friends and Thomas, but Katherine was nowhere to be found; as the kids and Thomas woke up in the middle of the street. They were in the dream world version of Clouds-dale and as all the kids woke up, they started to get worried. Thomas gets up saying, "Don't worry, kids, I'll protect you."

Frank replies with, "Don't worry we can handle ourselves." Marcus starts to laugh as an echo goes throughout the dream world as Thomas and the kids hear it and start to get a little scared. Thomas spots a figure in the distance as a shadow stands underneath a streetlight as the figure starts walking towards them. Thomas tells the kids to run as they follow Thomas into a building and block the door with whatever they could find. Turns out, they ran into Clouds-dale high school, where Marcus had some fond and fun memories. The kids finally settled down in a classroom where they make a small fort to hold of Marcus for now. Selena says, "Oh god, he'll be here any minute."

Roland starts thinking, and says, "We just have to have Katherine wake us up. That's the only way to get out of here."

Jack talks to Thomas, saying, "Any ideas?"

Thomas pulled out a candle and put it on the floor saying, "We can use this candle to help us escape."

Judy looks and says, "Great, anybody got marshmallows? 'Cause hubby over here has a candle."

"It's not just any candle though," says Thomas. "If I light this candle, we will have only twenty minutes to chant a saying that Katherine found a while back."

Jack looks at Thomas saying, "So, if you chant the chant, we all go to the real world again?"

Thomas says, "Yup, will be safe from Marcus then."

As Jack looks at his friends, saying, "Come guys, we got to distract Marcus, so he doesn't get to Thomas."

Marcus comes to the high school main entrance as he gets an evil looking smile on his face, knowing he is going to have some fun. Marcus kicks open the door like nothing, as all the stuff blocking it flies back down the hall. Marcus walks in seeing desks, tables, and broken wood planks everywhere, as he is ready to start his hunt for the kids and Thomas. Marcus hears the sound of a desk getting slid across the floor, so he goes to follow the sound. Kelly bumped into a desk saying, "Oh damn, he must have heard me," as she begins finding a hiding place. Roland and Frank were working on a trap for Marcus inside the auditorium; while Judy and Selena work on another trap inside the science lab.

Sandy steps out of a classroom just as Marcus gets closer to Kelly knowing full well, she couldn't defend herself. Sandy looks at Marcus and shouts at him saying, "Hey, you creepy, murderous, bastard, come get some of this if you want it." Marcus stops and turns around slowly, and the second he spots her he starts running really fast; as

Sandy starts to run as well, trying to get away. Marcus wants his gloves bad, and will do anything he can to get them. Marcus uses the spell dream power, as he takes his whole arm off and throws it at Sandy, making it a homing missile. Sandy tries to out run the arm by going into a classroom and closing the door and locking it. Marcus' arm was too strong for just a mere door to hold it back; as it burst through the door and grabbed Sandy by the neck, and pinned her against the wall.

Sandy struggled with the arm as Marcus came walking in and grew another arm out of the clear blue. Marcus says to Sandy, "So sweetie…any idea who has my gloves, my dear?" Sandy spits on Marcus and cries for help on the top of her lungs. No more than a second after she shouts does Marcus put his fist through her head and pulls out her brain. Marcus licks her brain as he then drops it, and steps on it like a bug, watching Sandy's corpse drop to the floor with nothing but a hole in her head. Marcus felt great as he felt the blood between his fingers, hoping to kill another. Marcus comes out of the classroom with a smile on his face as he is ready to hunt for yet another victim. Marcus hears glass break from another room that's down the hall, as he slowly heads that way to hopefully kill and take another soul. Marcus opens the door and see's that it's the science lab, and looks around to see who was there. Judy and Selena are both watching from inside the cabinet as they see Marcus get into the middle of the room. They spring the trap as they pull two strings to drop down homemade ice bombs that freeze Marcus in place. Judy and Selena get out of the cabinet as they try and get around Marcus. Marcus breaks out of the icy prison and throws shadow knifes at the two girls running to get out of the classroom. Selena ran out of the room as she headed to find another place to hide. Judy was not so lucky though; as she fell to Marcus' shadow daggers and landed on the floor, dead as a door nail. Marcus walks out of the science lab as he looks around and says, "Come out…come out…wherever you are." Marcus walks around in hopes of finding another kid. Frank and Roland get the trap ready for Marcus at the auditorium. Marcus hears sounds coming from the auditorium so he heads in to search for more victims to claim. Frank and Roland spot Marcus entering the auditorium, and so they waited for Marcus to get into place before springing their trap. Marcus looks around but finds no one in sight as he takes a second to look at his hands to watch the blood drip off from his recent kill. Frank looks at Roland and nods his head in a *yes* formation, that gives Roland the signal to activate the trap. Roland and Frank both release two huge, heavy punching bags as they swing down to Marcus' direction. Marcus hears something, as he turns around slowly to find two punching bags heading his way. Marcus is hit by the punching bags, as they send him flying through a brick wall. Frank and Roland make their way out of the auditorium while Marcus lays in a pile of brick and rubble for now.

The gang meets back up in the hall in the front room where they started at, as Thomas is almost done with the spell. They head in the room as they look around to see if everyone was here but right away, Jack and Jennifer notice a few people missing. Jack says, "Where's Sandy and Judy? Shouldn't they be with you guys?"

Selena says, "We tried to get him with a trap but he broke free too soon, and caught Judy before she could escape."

"Well, he didn't find me," said Bobby.

"Well, he came close to finding me," said Kelly. "But I was saved by Sandy; but Marcus killed her."

Jack gets pissed knowing two more of his friends are dead and now, he wants revenge.

"That bastard killed Judy and Sandy; we can't let him get away with this," said Jennifer.

The rest of the gang agrees while Roland responds with, "Me and Frank put him through a wall with a couple of punching bags. He should be out for, at least, a few seconds," said Frank.

They hear banging at the door, as a voice is heard mere seconds later, saying, "I hope one of you has my gloves 'cause if not, I'm gonna be real pissed; and then I start getting creative."

Thomas hurries up with the spell as the kids stand away from the door. Marcus busts down the door as he sees the kids in the corner and Thomas doing a chant; but he is unaware of the chant he knows. Marcus goes towards Thomas slowly, as Bobby takes a chair and rams it into Marcus' back; it pierces his spine. Marcus still stands after that attack and turns his head around as he holds him tight, getting ready to squeeze him to death. Marcus turns and says, "Give me the gloves or another friend of yours dies…NOW!"

Jack takes the gloves out of his backpack and holds them in his hands, saying, "Let him go and I'll give you your gloves."

Marcus replies with, "First, the gloves, and then you can get your friend back."

Jack thinks about the decision to give him the gloves; at the same time, he knows, despite his words, Marcus will still kill Bobby. Marcus lets go of Bobby and leaps over to Jack while the chair is still through his spine. Jack dodges out of the way, as do the rest of the kids, as they head over to Thomas to protect him. Marcus lays on the floor as he had crushed a table with his body and was now on top of it. Thomas says the last few words needed to get out of the dream world and wake up. Marcus, in a flash, quickly stretches out his right arm as he manages to grab the gloves from Jack's hands just as they wake up.

Marcus now has his two gloves, with blades located on each and every finger and thumb of the gloves, and he can't wait to start using them again. The gang wake up with headaches as the spell had a slight side effect, which were massive headaches; to which, Thomas takes out some aspirin and gives it to the kids with a full blown up bottle of water. The kids have their pill and their drink of water as they try regain their focus and balance, as they try to get up on their two feet. Marcus on the other hand awoke with a murderous feeling of joy, as he now goes out into Clouds-dale looking for someone to tear apart. Katherine helps the kids and her husband Thomas up off the ground, as it does not take them long to get back on track. Katherine is worried as she does not see the gloves anywhere in sight; which leads her to believe Marcus has the gloves. Jack looks to Katherine and says, "Sorry, he grabbed them from us at the last second; just before we woke up." Katherine tells the kids to get inside the car as well as her husband Thomas. Thomas is worried himself as he can only dread to what Marcus will do now that he has the gloves. Marcus comes across a couple wandering in the street of Clouds-dale; late after leaving a dance club. Marcus sparred no time waiting, as he sprung out like a cat; only for his claw to pierce the man's chest in the middle of the street. The girl screams and runs off down the street as she is horrified at the sight of her date being impaled. Marcus shreds his claws through his body like a shredder, as the man's screams of pain wake up the neighborhood. Marcus finishes him with his index blade going through his nose and cutting a circle in his skull on the other side, as a brain just falls out of his head. Marcus takes the brain and throws it at the girl that ran. The girl is hit by the brain, as Marcus runs after her the second she hits the ground. Marcus had never run this fast before; it was though he was hungry for human blood. Marcus catches up with the girl, as he goes ahead and thrusts his claws into her body as it pierced her neck and into her brain. The girl leaks blood out of her neck, slowly, as Marcus licks the blood off his claws and gets up slowly; now ready to kill another victim.

Katherine is still worried and tries to come up with a solution to try and stop Marcus. Jack and Jennifer talk to Katherine and say, "Isn't there anyone that can help us?" said Jack.

"There has to be someone who you know that can help us stop Marcus?" said Jennifer. Katherine knows two people who can help, but never mentions them because she wants them out of Marcus' life forever.

Thomas does the honors instead as Katherine is unaware to what Thomas is about to say. "We can go see Billy and Summer 'cause we need all the help we can get right now," said Thomas.

Jack and the other kids now had an even bigger question mark above their heads as Bobby says, "Who's Billy and Summer?"

Katherine steps in before Thomas could say a word, "They're no one right now. So, don't worry about it."

Katherine thinks of a plan and says, "I have an idea; there is a spell I have located in a box at a bank, that should be able to stop Marcus." Katherine and the others get into the car; they drive to the National Cloud Bank. Katherine gets out of the car and dashes to the back of the bank. Thomas and others try to keep up as Katherine is already picking the lock.

Roland looks at Katherine and says, "Are you crazy? We're breaking into a bank. You're going to get us arrested." Katherine gets the door unlocked just mere seconds after Roland spoke. Katherine heads in quietly as she works her way to the safe; to where the guard there is just beginning to check is round in the safe. Katherine sneaks to the guard's location and dodges the guard's flashlight and eyesight, as she manages to get in the vault. Katherine unlocks her box and grabs a very particular stack of cash and heads out.

Thomas and the others see Katherine come out of the bank unharmed and with a stack of hundreds in her hand. Thomas and the kids head back to the car with Katherine as they head off into Clouds-dale to locate Marcus. Jack asks, "So what where's this spell you said you were getting? 'Cause all I see is a nice, fat stack of cash."

Frank replies with, "Maybe we're going to bribe Marcus, I guess. I don't know."

"No kids, I'm sorry but money doesn't seem to interest Marcus," said Katherine. "Don't worry, I have the spell but we have to find Marcus though,"

"But what spell is it if you don't mind us asking?" said Selena.

Katherine thinks before talking and says, "It's a binding spell—and a powerful one at that; so, it should hold Marcus in place for a while."

Kelly scratches her head and says, "A binding spell? What's that?"

Well it's a spell that binds the victim to anything the user says; it is bound to," says Katherine.

Thomas looks back at the kids and says, "Yup, don't worry, this spell should hold Marcus for good."

Katherine drives around searching for Marcus, unaware that Marcus is close. Marcus finds that a window is slightly open as he heads over to it, finding a bunch of kids on the floor, drunk and tired, as they just got done partying. Marcus finds this to be the perfect chance for some fun. Marcus opens the window and sneak's in as the kids in the house were unaware of his presence. Marcus goes in the kitchen and finds lighter fluid; as he gets an evil idea.

Marcus starts squirting lighter fluid all over the kids as they are still passed out. He continues to do it more and more as he locks all the doors and windows in the house afterwards. Marcus then turns off the water to the sink in the kitchen as he grabs a lighter in a drawer. Marcus heads to the back door and locks it while it is open, and lights the lighter, only to throw it on a seventeen-year-old boy as he sets him on fire. Marcus quickly locks the door and slams it as he watches the fun begin. Marcus stood there as the seventeen-year-old boy ran as he was screaming in pain since his body was almost completely on fire. The boy ran into another boy, and another, and a few girls while he was at it. Each boy and girl in there were lit on fire due to the lighter fluid Marcus had sprayed on them. The screams were so loud and fierce that Katherine heard them as she was driving just a block away. Katherine listened, saying, "Marcus has already started. Quick; we have to hurry," as Katherine raced to the house. In the time between the cry for help and Katherine arriving at the house; the house was half way ablaze. The fire department sirens were near as the neighbor across the street had made the call. Katherine and Thomas jumped out of the car as they told the kids to stay in the car. Katherine's eyes were wide open as though she's seeing it all again for the first time. She's horrified that Marcus is doing it all again as she cries running towards the house to help the kids, but Thomas stops her in time as he had spotted Marcus.

"Look, there he is, Katherine!" shouts Thomas, as they chase after him. Marcus spots them as well and starts running as he wants to have a little fun before killing his own sister and her husband. Marcus turns a corner and around a fence figuring she would follow right behind him. Katherine, instead, comes up to the next street and sees Marcus from a far, as she holds up the spell in her hand, ready to conjuror up the spell.

Katherine starts chanting the binding spell as Marcus is aware of the particular spell she's using. Marcus hears the chant and remembers it as though he had said it yesterday. Marcus says the spell better and faster than Katherine as it came back to him. Marcus finishes the spell before Katherine as he binds her to that exact location she is standing on. Katherine cannot move from the area she is bound to, for if she goes outside the limit of the binding spell, she will die. Katherine is surround by a bright purple circle as it is binding circle to the spell. The kids get out of the car and see for themselves that Thomas cannot free her; nor can the kids.

Marcus sees a garbage truck up ahead as he runs to it as fast as possible before Thomas finds a way to reverse the spell. Katherine tells Thomas, "The only way to the break the spell is to destroy the object that I'm bound too." Katherine was standing in the middle of the street as Marcus had just reached the garbage truck and started to hot-wire it the second he had got in. Frank spots a construction truck no more than half a block away, as he tells Roland and Bobby to follow him. Frank, Roland and Bobby get to the construction truck; when they get to the construction truck, they find a jackhammer in the back of truck. They get out of the construction truck and run over to Katherine with the jackhammer. They set down a battery pack to plug into the jackhammer as Thomas picks up the jackhammer and places it at the spot where Katherine is standing. Katherine moves just enough for Thomas to use the jackhammer so she doesn't get hurt. Thomas starts up the jackhammer, as Marcus manages to hot wire the garbage truck. Thomas starts hammering the spot where Katherine is standing, as Marcus starts revving up the truck and is ready to run over Katherine. Before Marcus could run over Katherine with the garbage truck, Thomas rescues her by destroying the spot where Katherine was standing. Once the spell was broken, Thomas picked up Katherine and moved her out of the way just before Marcus could run them over. Marcus was mad; he missed Katherine and was unaware he was about to drive into a cement wall. Marcus crashes into the wall sending him flying through the windshield and into the wall. Thomas, Katherine and the kids find somewhere to hide, so they hide inside in an abandoned warehouse. Katherine tells Thomas to stay with the kids so she can use the binding spell on Marcus without putting the kids in harm's way. Katherine runs to the crash site where Marcus hit the wall; she almost tires herself out from the sprinting. Marcus had left the truck already and was trying to escape before Katherine could put the spell on him. Katherine gets to the truck as she takes deep breaths when she arrives; as she needed to catch her breath from the running she was doing.

Having no time to herself, she looked inside and noticed Marcus was gone and immediately, she starts looking everywhere for him since he couldn't have gotten far. Marcus held his side with his right arm; as his left side ribs were hurting from the crash. No less than a block away, Marcus was slowly running down another street so he could hide and heal from his current injury. Katherine looked down the street he was on and saw him as she starts running at him; full force, as though she gained the energy out of nowhere.

Katherine was able to catch up to Marcus as he breaks into a butcher shop and tries to hide. Katherine was able to reach a point where she jump-kicked Marcus through a door and landed onto the floor. Now, Katherine had her chance as she chants the spell, saying every word right and on point. She finishes the spell, binding Marcus to that exact spot on the floor where he was laying. A light-purple circle glowing around Marcus appears as he now is bound to that very circle and cannot leave it or else, he will die. Katherine turns around and walks away in relief as she heads back to the abandoned warehouse to tell her husband and the kids the good news. Katherine tries to take small breaths as she needed to catch her breath; since she was running like hell to catch Marcus. Thomas and the others hear a knock on the warehouse door as Selena and Kelly jump at the sound of the knocking; believing it was Marcus. Thomas just knew it had to be Katherine, as his heart raced fast; hoping it wasn't Marcus; hoping to see Katherine. Thomas slightly opened the door and saw a smile on Katherine's face as he opened the door wide and hugged her with passion; thanking the lord she was not dead. Katherine told her husband and the kids about what happened, Selena had a few questions as to how she managed to get him. "How did you manage to put the spell on Marcus?" said Selena.

"Well, I ran after him and into the back room of a butcher shop and managed to kick him to the ground," replied Katherine. "It helped the fact he was already hurt from the crash, so I guess I just finished the job and afterwards. I said the spell and boom, got him bound to the spot where he laid on the floor," said Katherine.

Jack wanted to know where the butcher shop was so he could finish Marcus off once and for all. Jack asked Katherine, saying, "Where is this shop? I have to know."

Katherine replied, "Yeah, don't worry I just have to catch my breath."

Roland agreed with Jack, saying, "Yeah, let's go now otherwise he might wake up and find a way to escape."

Frank, Selena, Kelly, Jennifer, and Bobby agree as well, as they were ready and willing to go get Marcus and to try to find a way to kill him. Thomas stops the kids, saying, "If you go now, he's just going to use you to set him free or worse: Kill another one of you and greater his chances of surviving longer."

Jack runs out before Thomas could finish as he tries to find the butcher shop on his own. Thomas and the others shout, "WAIT, JACK!" as everyone runs after him as he goes down the exact street where Katherine chased down Marcus. Jack finds a butcher shop while running as he runs right; in trying to find Marcus before he escapes. Jack finds the back room, where he finds Marcus standing there, as he had woken up from Katherine knocking him out.

Marcus stands there smiling as he sees Jack right in front of him, but is just out of reach of his gloves for him to grab and kill him. Marcus says, "So it's one of the college boys who has come to kill me huh? I didn't know my sister hired such pathetic college kids to kill me."

Jack says, "We're here to do a report on you. That's it, so back off on us man, okay? You've killed enough of my friends already."

Marcus looks at him with an even more sinister look, saying with a smile, "I've only just begun you little bitch.

You're nothing more than a piece of meat for my claws to turn you into shredded red puddles of shit and blood," as he shows him the book titled *Dark Power.*

Katherine and the others arrive as he just pulls out the book. "Jack stay back," says Katherine.

Marcus replies, "Well, sister, now how did you know that I like gifts?"

Katherine now has a question mark on top of her head wondering what he's talking about, saying, "Marcus stop playing games I didn't give you anything." Marcus shows her the binding spell she had in her hands before; but now Marcus has it, as he puts it back into his book. Marcus see's the page fuse with the book as it has been returned to its proper place, making Marcus just one step closer to being back to his powerful wicked self.

Katherine replies with, "How did you get that?"

"Simple, my dear," says Marcus. "When you attacked me, I managed to pry it from your lovely hands, my sweet sister." She was outraged Marcus outsmarted her; and was mad at herself at the same time. Marcus is aware that they're trying to find a way to kill him by means of physically, or magically; either way, Marcus must die. Marcus stood there in his circle as he knows how to escape; it's just a matter of when he will choose to.

I'm going to teach you, brother, that you should not fuck with me 'cause I will send your sorry ass to hell, you mass murdering bastard," Katherine shouts out. She immediately ran out into the street and found a truck to which she broke into and hotwired it. Katherine was ready to drive through the wall, as the group comes out of the butcher shop watching Katherine run into the wall to kill

Marcus. She revs up the truck, as she punches it and runs the truck into the wall, bringing down the wall on top of Marcus. Thomas runs to the truck to see if Katherine is okay, and of course she was, as her husband helps her out of the busted-up truck. Jack looked down at the pile feeling satisfied that Marcus was gone.

The rest of the crew felt the exact same way as they gathered in a group with Jack saying, "I'm glad that's over, maybe now we have enough on our report to get an $A+$."

Roland couldn't think about the report, all he could think about were his friends that were murdered. Katherine and her husband Thomas walked the kids back to their house after a long day of horror and death. They arrived home safely, as Katherine for some reason, was on edge thinking Marcus was always right behind her. Thomas went in the house with the kids as he made them some hot chocolate, as he said to Katherine, "Honey, calm down, Marcus isn't going to bother the kids anymore."

Jennifer looks at her friends and says, "Well, we did it, guys. We stopped that magical psychopath once and for all."

Roland started to shed a tear, as he said to his friends, "I was going to ask Sandy to the dance party we were having this weekend at the college. But all that went out the window when Marcus killed her and now, I feel alone again," said Roland.

Jack sits next to Roland, saying, "Hey, don't worry man, we'll find you someone for the dance." Jack looks down and says, "Right now, we have to notify the parents and let them know what happened." Frank receives his hot chocolate from Thomas as he sips it and enjoys the taste of the hot coco Thomas had prepared for him.

Frank smiled in a warm manner, as he got relaxed in the seat he was sitting in. Frank then noticed everyone getting up and started to walk downstairs into Katherine and Thomas' basement; to which he was wondering to where everyone was going. Frank got up as he followed them to see why they were all of a sudden heading downstairs to the basement, as he still had a question mark over his head. Frank continued to head downstairs when he started to see everyone in red robes with torches with a table as though they were about to perform a ritual. Frank drops the hot coco and says, "What the fuck is going on here, guys?" They all turn to him as he tries to go back upstairs; and finds out the door is locked, as the figures in red robes came up stairs to get him as he screams, "AH! Get away from me!" They take him over to the table and put him on it as he still screams in horror as he is now scared to death to what is happening. Frank gets tied to the table as he is gagged, while he is still screaming intensely. Frank looked over to the right of him and saw an executioner-like figure come out of the shadows with a big axe. Frank's nerves are shot at this point, meanwhile everyone in the group sees frank starting to shake uncontrollably in his sleep.

Jack shakes and slaps Frank as he is trying to wake him up. The executioner lifts up his axe, as he slams it down and strikes Frank with it; it cuts him in half leaving him only half the man he is. Jack leaped off Frank as he is split in half in real life with no blood coming out of him. Jack and everyone else stood in silence as they wanted to scream but were too afraid to do it. Katherine and Thomas walked in as they see the horror that is Frank's body cut in half lying on the living room carpet. Katherine knew right away she didn't kill Marcus; it was too easy to believe it was all over. She should have known that Marcus wasn't going down without a fight. *But how?* Katherine wondered, *how could he have gotten away from me when I know I crushed him?*

Jack and the others were very wide awake as they planned on not going to sleep for a very long time or at least, until their body gives out and they pass out. Thomas had to think of something that would help keep the kids awake, so he ran upstairs to find something he hid in case of situations like this. Roland as well as everyone else tries to come up with a plan to stop Marcus before someone ends up becoming the next victim.

Meanwhile, Marcus had located Katherine's house and was sneaking around outside to see if there were any easy access points for getting into the house unnoticed. Marcus had a nice little distraction for them, as he took his gloves and carved his name in the fence out in the backyard as he sprayed gasoline on it and lit it on fire.

Marcus leaves the fire burning as he sneaks around hoping to get in unnoticed from there and getting the rest of his pages back to put into his book. Katherine went back into the kitchen to get something to drink; as it helps her think in times like this. Katherine takes out a bottle of wine vintage 1914 as she gets a wine glass along with it. She opens the bottle and before she starts to pour the wine, she notices on the corner of her eye a bright glow of fire. She drops the bottle of wine as it shatters upon impact hitting the floor while she runs to the window. The kids and her husband race to the kitchen to see what happened and to see if Katherine was alright. When everyone arrived in the kitchen, their mouths were as open, as Katherine was staring out the window seeing Marcus Slayer's name as it was on fire and starting to burn down the property. Marcus laughs in the house as it comes from the living room. Everyone's eyes widened with fear as they saw him walk into the kitchen doorway. Marcus shows Katherine his book; he has more pages in his book then he did before. "Ha ha ha ha," chuckles Marcus. Did you really think you could keep me away from my pages forever, sis? I found all the pages you hid here in the house but I know you have the rest somewhere else, right?" said Marcus. "So just tell me where they are and I'll spare the kids' lives for the rest of the evening, and leave them alone," said Marcus seriously. Marcus slides his claw gloves along the wall as they rip through the wall as though it was paper. "But if you don't tell me where the rest of the pages are, then I'm afraid I'll just have to kill every, single, last, one of them, until you CAVE!"

Katherine and Thomas get the kids out of the house but Bobby and Kelly stay in the house holding kitchen knives in their hands. Thomas shouts, "COME ON; NOW IS NOT THE TIME TO FIGHT!" Kelly throws her knife into Marcus' upper leg as Bobby threw his into his right arm. Marcus screamed in pain for a second as he falls to the floor watching blood come from his leg and arm. Katherine and the others watched as he fell, Kelly grabs another kitchen knife, ready to kill him with the finishing blow. Marcus takes out the knifes in his body slowly as he gets up in a matter of seconds.

Kelly throws the knife once more at Marcus, but Marcus smacks it aside with his gloves. Marcus threw the two kitchen knives at Kelly and Bobby and had got both of them in the knee cap causing them to fall instantly. "AHHHH!" Kelly and Bobby screamed as they cried in agony, as Marcus walks over to Bobby and runs his claws into his face having the blades run through his skull. Marcus pulls his head off with one tug of strength and throws it in the trash.

Marcus laughs in a sinister manner, "Ha ha ha ha…he was trash anyway. Speaking of trash…" Marcus turns his sights to Kelly, to which at this point, Thomas and the others started to carry her out. Thomas carries Kelly and runs along with everyone else, as they race to the cars. Marcus comes out of the house and pulls out his spell book. Marcus opens up the book and locates a spell that's perfect for this situation. "The soft touch spell," Marcus whispered to himself, as he started to cast the spell saying the words as they were written. Thomas and the others are getting close to the cars but will they get there in time before Marcus can finish? Marcus says the last of the words and finishes the spell just as everyone gets to the cars.

Nothing happens right away as Thomas puts Kelly in Selena's car. Thomas and the others ride in Katherine's car as they drive out of there. Marcus walks along the streets as Katherine's property burns more and more, as it starts to burn to her house. Katherine drove ahead of Selena so she could follow her to a safe location.

Unaware, Selena was in grave danger, being in the same car as Kelly, as nothing was wrong with her, but the soft touch spell makes anyone explode with the slightest, hard tap. Just then, Kelly had to sneeze so hard, she jolted back hitting the seat hard enough for her to explode; taking the car and Selena with her.

# Chapter 4
## Unforgiving Intentions

Katherine stepped on the brake hard enough to put her foot through the floor of the car. She was screaming, "NOOOO, DAMN YOU, MARCUS!" as she could do nothing more than watch Selena's body burn; as it was thrown from the car explosion and into the street. Jack, Jennifer, and Roland where the last of the group of kids who started the report and said a prayer for both Kelly and Selena. Jack, Jennifer, and Roland all decided this had to end tonight, for they realized if they're going to die, they will choose when, not Marcus. Katherine got back in the car after she had finished drying up her tears for Selena and Kelly. "We're ending this tonight, Katherine, I think it's time we give Marcus a proper welcoming back party," Jack said.

Thomas looks back at Jack and says, "You got a plan to go with that idea?"

"Yes, as a matter of fact, we do," replies Roland as they drive off to the location where the rest of the pages are.

Katherine continues to drive as she has quite a bit of driving to go still. "So, what exactly do you have planned for Marcus next time you see him?" said Katherine.

"Well, for one, we use his own magic against him to hold him at bay and second, we try and get the book from him so we can magically disarm him," says Jack.

"Yeah, then we use his own magic to physically disarm him and then once he's fully disarmed, we kill him once and for all," says Roland. Thomas likes the idea and so does Katherine, but the one thing they're all thinking is, *It's not going to be that easy.* Meanwhile, Marcus walks in the same direction as Katherine but is not even close to their location yet. Marcus pulls out the book and opens it up and searches for a spell to help. Marcus finds one called earth mover and so, starts reading the incantation to cast it. Earth mover allowed the user to move the earth under his feet and made him go faster, or higher than the ground level, or lower then ground level; allowing no harm to come to him while underground. Marcus finishes the spell but nothing happened until he started raising his right hand. Marcus raises his right hand slowly and notices he is becoming taller and then lowers his right hand to see he's getting shorter. Marcus realized his right hand controlled the earth and so he picked it up slowly, and kept it straight out and noticed he's moving forward. Katherine continues to drive to the location to where the rest of the pages are; which they are getting closer. Katherine says, "You kids doing okay back there? 'Cause it's not much further now."

Jennifer replies, "So where exactly are the rest of the pages."

Thomas replied to Jennifer, saying, "They're very well hidden on top of the clock tower in the center of the town; so, that's where we must go." Not too far behind them is Marcus who is surfing the earth under his feet as he moves fast enough to start playing catch up to Katherine. Marcus, standing there as his right hand controls the earth under him, thinks to himself, *I wonder where that bitch put the rest of my pages.* Marcus knew he had a good few spells but none of the fun ones, including the one that allows him to create fire out of nowhere. Katherine and the others finally arrived at the clock tower to which they get out in a hurry, and noticed that Marcus was nowhere in sight. They take this time to head inside the clock tower and start making their way up the stairs.

Marcus closes in on their location trying to find their whereabouts as he starts looking around as he surfs the streets of Clouds-dale. Marcus happens to spot the color of a car from the corner of his right eye. This color was the same as Katherine's car, which is an off-white color, so he heads in that direction to see if it is her car, indeed. Marcus arrives at the car only to find out it was actually her car that's parked in front of the clock tower. Marcus put his right hand down and evened out the pavement of the street to return it to normal.

Then he reversed the spell, bringing the pavement right back to an even state.

Marcus walks in the clock tower only to hear the sound of footsteps going up the stairs. Katherine, Thomas and the kids continue hiking their way up the stairs which were now proving to be tiring and tedious. A chill goes up their spine when they hear the sound of metal claws shrieking up against wall. Marcus' voice travels through the clock tower, saying, "Run as fast as you can…'cause when I catch you…I'll cut your bleeding heart right out of your DAMN CHEST! Ha ha ha ha," Marcus chuckled through the tower. Katherine and the others move quickly as they can see the end of the stairs far up ahead but still, it gave them hope knowing they were almost there. Marcus shrieks his claws against the walls as the sound gets louder and louder. The group gets a little nervous now as he should not be gaining as quickly as he is. Katherine and the others manage to make it to the top as they get out of the tower stairway and outside on top of the roof of the clock tower itself.

Katherine, right away, runs to a brick on the corner of the edge as Marcus manages to get to the top, as his head creeps up the stairs. Marcus make a vicious smirk as he says, "Fee fie foe fom. I smell the fear of little bitches on the top of the chicken-shit clock tower."

Jack, Roland, and Jennifer move to the side as Thomas hides behind the tower itself as he slides around it. Marcus appears in the moonlight as he sees Katherine in his sights and notices the kids on the right. Marcus walks out slowly as he stops midway and sees Katherine by the corner of the edge of the rooftop. "So…where are they?" says Marcus in a voice that sends a chill up his own sister's spine. Marcus walks closer to Katherine as he gets closer and closer to her, as she gets a little more scared backing up to where she feels the bricks against her back. Marcus slides one blade along the bricks, as it makes a sound that sends more chills up Katherine's spine. Marcus stops as he is only a foot away from Katherine.

Katherine looks at Marcus in his eyes and says, "Why are you doing this again, Marcus? Stop this already I'm not giving you the pages!" Marcus grabs Katherine by the throat as he slowly slides his index claw to her heart, as he presses a little hard against her as she starts to bleed.

Marcus whispers to Katherine, "Tell Thomas to come out with my pages before we have a very serious heart to heart talk about your life."

Thomas comes out shouting, "OKAY! Fine, I'll come out, just stop hurting her." Thomas shows himself to Marcus as Marcus looks at him with deadly intentions.

"Okay, hero, let's go hand over the pages, or you can kiss Katherine goodbye," said Marcus.

Thomas said, "Fine, I'll give them to you but please don't hurt her anymore." Thomas heads over to a brick located above the doorway by the staircase entrance.

Marcus watches as he sees him carefully making sure he doesn't make any sudden movements; besides getting him what he wants. Thomas takes a brick out of the wall, as it was a fake brick designed to hide anything of value, and wouldn't you know it, the last of the pages were there. Marcus slowly walks over to Thomas with Katherine close to him to make sure he still gives him what he wants; or else he will make Katherine into shredded pieces of flesh. Thomas hands the pages over to him as he throws Katherine over to Thomas, who catches her in the process. Marcus takes the pages and tries to combine the pages into the book to which they did not go and latch on like the other pages. Marcus looked at the pages and saw they were not the exact original pages of the book but copies made by a printer. By the time Marcus realized it, Jack had found, and is now saying, the incantation for a spell called levitating palm. This spell allows the user to grab any item with a ghost hand and take things, and can bring them to him through solid objects. Jack had finished the spell and surprisingly had said it perfectly. Marcus looked at Katherine and Thomas and said, "So you think I'm playing around, huh?" Marcus tears up the paper as he throws it in the air and shreds it up so much, that by the time it flies away, it looks like confetti. Marcus says, "I think I'll kill you first, Thomas. I'll save Katherine for…" just then the book was grabbed from Marcus' hands. Jack had performed the spell successfully, and had managed to grab the book from Marcus; as they get it and use the ghost hand to push Marcus off the clock tower as he falls 300 ft straight down to the ground. Marcus hit the ground so hard it cracked the pavement, leaving an indent. Katherine, Thomas and the kids headed down the stairs, to see it for their own eyes, to see if Marcus Slayer had truly died. If so, this would be the end to a very long and horrifying night of terror.

They took five minutes to come down the stairs of the clock tower, so somewhere in manner of five minutes, Marcus got up and walked away as though it didn't bother him. Marcus was then spotted walking down the street, heading their way. Jack looks up another spell since the levitating palm spell had run out. Jack looked and found a damnation spell; it would send a soul to hell and trap them there. But the problem is the incantation was long and some words were hard to pronounce. Jack said, "You guys try to buy some time. If I can get this incantation done, we can end this." Jack ran inside the building to try and buy time, as the other would keep him busy. Thomas and Katherine found themselves a metal pipe and rusty sharp piece of metal. Jennifer and Roland found a car door opened; they tried to hotwire the car so they could use it against Marcus.

Katherine gets ready, as does Thomas, as Marcus gets closer; he is only ten-feet away. Marcus stops as he looks at them with a smile and killing urge in his eye. "Don't you get tired of trying to kill me…I mean honestly, I'm well protected cause as long as that book has a connection with me, I won't die unless you kill me with a spell." Marcus makes a serious face saying, "Now move, the both of you, I have a kid to kill and turn him into nothing more than blood stain on my shirt." Katherine and Thomas rush at him as they swing left and right as Marcus blocked the attacks coming in one after the other with his claws still attached. Katherine turned her body to swing so hard, she not only broke off the claws on his right hand, but broke his hand in the process. Marcus, although injured, swiped with the claw on his left hand and slashed through the pipe and the metal shard. Marcus kicks down Thomas; only slashed his arm bad, causing it to bleed. Katherine tried to attack Marcus for hurting Thomas, but Marcus knocked her down as well; doing nothing but putting a few scrapes on her arm and leg. "Now if you'll excuse me, I have to…" just then, BEEP, BEEP! a car smacks into Marcus, sending him flying into another car, as it explodes on contact. Katherine and the others stood and watched as Marcus was burned in the fire. Marcus got up no more than thirty seconds later, as he shakes off the fire like its dust. Marcus looks at them as he heals the bones in his hand as he runs, now going into the building to where Jack is, as they try to stop him. Marcus runs in as he hears Jack, so he follows his voice, as Jack sees Marcus and goes and runs from him as he continues to read the incantation. Marcus spots him as he runs faster, trying to catch up as Jack sees him and stops reading; only runs just as fast as Marcus, but away from him. Jack dodges in a dark spot located in the corner of a hall, as Marcus flies by him, not realizing he had passed him up. Jack continued the incantation as Marcus heard the words echo through the hall, as he looks and sees Jack in the corner now as he runs at him. Before Jack could get away, he throws him to the floor as the book goes further than him.

Marcus walks slowly to Jack saying, "You know you have just a few minutes to continue the incantation, before you have to restart it, ha ha ha ha," chuckles Marcus. Jack slides back trying to reach for the book as Marcus comes closer and closer. Marcus looks at Jack saying, as his claws scratch the wall, "Well, you came, you tried, you…failed," as his claw swipes of the wall. Marcus gets ready to slash Jack, as he grabs the book and blocks the attack with the book; took very little damage. Jack said the last of the words of the incantation of the damnation spell as the spell activates right away. Marcus screamed, "NOO! It can't be true; you get the spell off…" as hellfire came up from the ground to swirl around Marcus Slayer, as he looks around in fear not knowing what to do.

Just then Roland, Jennifer and the others came in as Jack yells, "Watch out!"

Marcus grabs Roland by the collar, dragging him in, as Jennifer, Thomas, and Katherine try to pull him out. Marcus looks at them saying, "I'll be back; just you wait, Jack. This ain't over, not by a long shot." Just like that, Marcus had been pulled into the fiery pits along with

Roland. His flesh had been torn off from his body and left as a bloody rag on the ground; as he was sent to hell along with Marcus.

"NOOOO!! ROLAND!" Jennifer and Jack said at the same time as tears ran down their cheeks for their good friend Roland.

Katherine and Thomas hugged and said sorry for all that the kids had gone through, and knew that there was nothing they could do to help cheer them up. Katherine looked at them and said, "Well, at least it's over. I'm just sorry it costed so many lives but it will be okay in the long-run."

Jack and Jennifer walked of and went back home, only to tell the tale to the town of Clouds-dale; where everyone will remember the day Marcus Slayer had come back.

# The Epilogue

The legend of Marcus Slayer will continue to haunt the minds of many, and put fear in those who had none. Marcus now lies trapped in hell, and is now hungry for revenge; if only he can find a way out of Hell. But let it be known to the reader: MARCUS SLAYER WILL RETURN!

THE END.
THANK YOU FOR READING!